Based on the TV series *SpongeBob SquarePants*™ created by Stephen Hillenburg as seen on Nickelodeon™

SIMON SPOTLIGHT/NICKELODEON

An imprint of Simon & Schuster Children's Publishing Division   New York London Toronto Sydney   1230 Avenue of the Americas, New York, New York 10020

For information about special discounts for bulk purchases, please contact Simon & Schuster Special Sales at 1-866-506-1949 or business@simonandschuster.com.
Manufactured in the United States 0611 LAK
First Edition
2 4 6 8 10 9 7 5 3 1
ISBN 978-1-4424-2088-5   These titles were previously published individually by Simon Spotlight.

SpongeBob
and the
Princess

by David Lewman

illustrated by Clint Bond

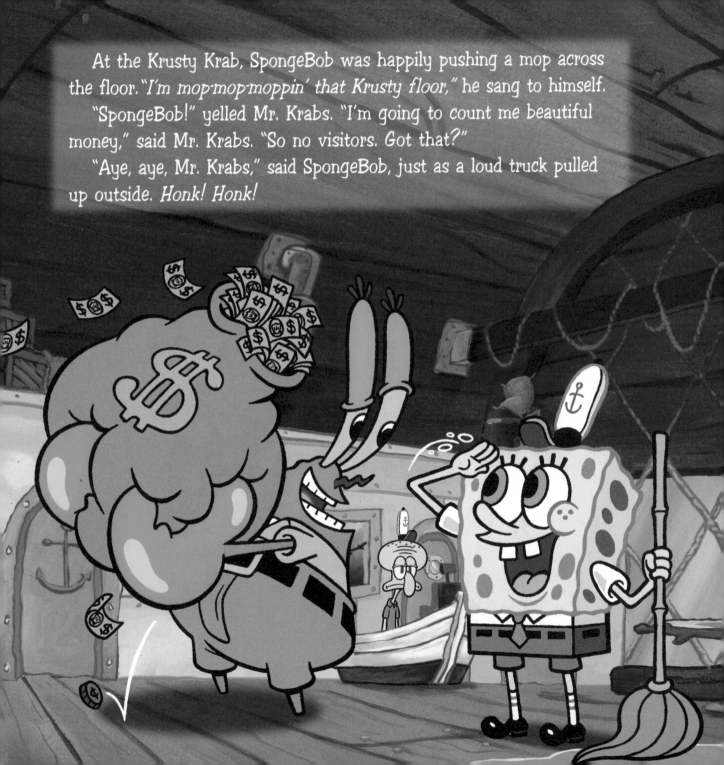

At the Krusty Krab, SpongeBob was happily pushing a mop across the floor. "*I'm mop-mop-moppin' that Krusty floor,*" he sang to himself.

"SpongeBob!" yelled Mr. Krabs. "I'm going to count me beautiful money," said Mr. Krabs. "So no visitors. Got that?"

"Aye, aye, Mr. Krabs," said SpongeBob, just as a loud truck pulled up outside. *Honk! Honk!*

"Welcome to the outside of the Krusty Krab. May I help you?" SpongeBob shouted to the driver, trying to make himself heard over the noise of the truck.

"Where's Mr. Krabs?" the driver asked.

"Counting his money, so he's not to be disturbed," answered SpongeBob. "Maybe I can help you."

"What?" yelled the driver.

SpongeBob cupped his hands to his mouth. "Maybe I can help you!"

"Tell Mr. Krabs that Princess Napkins will be here tomorrow," said the driver.

"What?" yelled SpongeBob.

"Princess delivery will be here tomorrow!" the driver shouted back.

"Got it!" said SpongeBob, giving a big thumbs-up. The driver drove off. "Hoppin' clams," said SpongeBob. "Wait till Squidward hears this!"

SpongeBob burst into the Krusty Krab. "Guess what,
Squidward! A princess'll be here tomorrow!"

Squidward didn't look up. "What princess would be caught dead in this dump?"
he asked gloomily. But then he brightened. "Unless it's . . . Princess Neptuna!
It doesn't seem likely, but for once, SpongeBob, I believe you! I *love* royalty!
They're so . . . *royal!*"

SpongeBob grinned. "I can't wait to tell Patrick and Sandy and Mrs. Puff and–"

Squidward shook his head. "No, no, don't tell anyone. Royal people love their privacy." Squidward figured he had a much better chance of getting Princess Neptuna's autograph if no one else was around.

"Really?" said SpongeBob, puzzled. "I thought princesses *loved* crowds."

Squidward sniffed. "You commoner. You know nothing about royalty."

SpongeBob thought hard. "Well, I *have* to tell Mr. Krabs."

"No!" yelled Squidward. "He'll ruin everything."

"But, Squidward," said SpongeBob, "it's my duty as a Krusty Krab employee!"

Squidward put his arm around SpongeBob. "Listen, SpongeBob," he said, "would you like me to teach you how to behave around royalty?"

SpongeBob's eyes grew big. "You'd teach me, Squidward?"

"Of course," said Squidward, smiling.

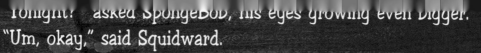

"Tonight?" asked SpongeBob, his eyes growing even bigger.

"Um, okay," said Squidward.

"At your house?" SpongeBob's eyes were huge. "With snacks?"

Squidward swallowed hard. "Sure, SpongeBob. I'm . . . inviting you . . . to my house . . . for royalty lessons and . . . snacks."

"HOORAY!" SpongeBob shouted. "I'll be there! And tomorrow the princess will be here!"

In his office Mr. Krabs heard SpongeBob shouting. "Better see what me employees are up to," he said, hurrying over to a picture on the wall. He lifted it and peered through a peephole just in time to hear SpongeBob say, "Tomorrow the princess will be here!"

"Princess?" whispered Mr. Krabs. "Princesses are rich! And people love to see 'em. People who could be MY PAYING CUSTOMERS! All I have to do is let everybody know a princess is coming to the Krusty Krab tomorrow! Hmm . . ."

That night Squidward tried to teach SpongeBob how to act properly around a princess. "No, no, SpongeBob," he scolded. "Never giggle when you bow to Princess Neptuna."

"But, Squidward," said SpongeBob. "I can't help it. Patrick looks kinda funny."

Patrick adjusted his crown. "Gee, thanks a lot, SpongeBob," he said. "I think I look beautiful."

Meanwhile Mr. Krabs was busy putting up signs all over Bikini Bottom announcing Princess Neptuna's arrival at the Krusty Krab. He chuckled to himself. "This ought to bring in the customers," he said. "*And their money!*"

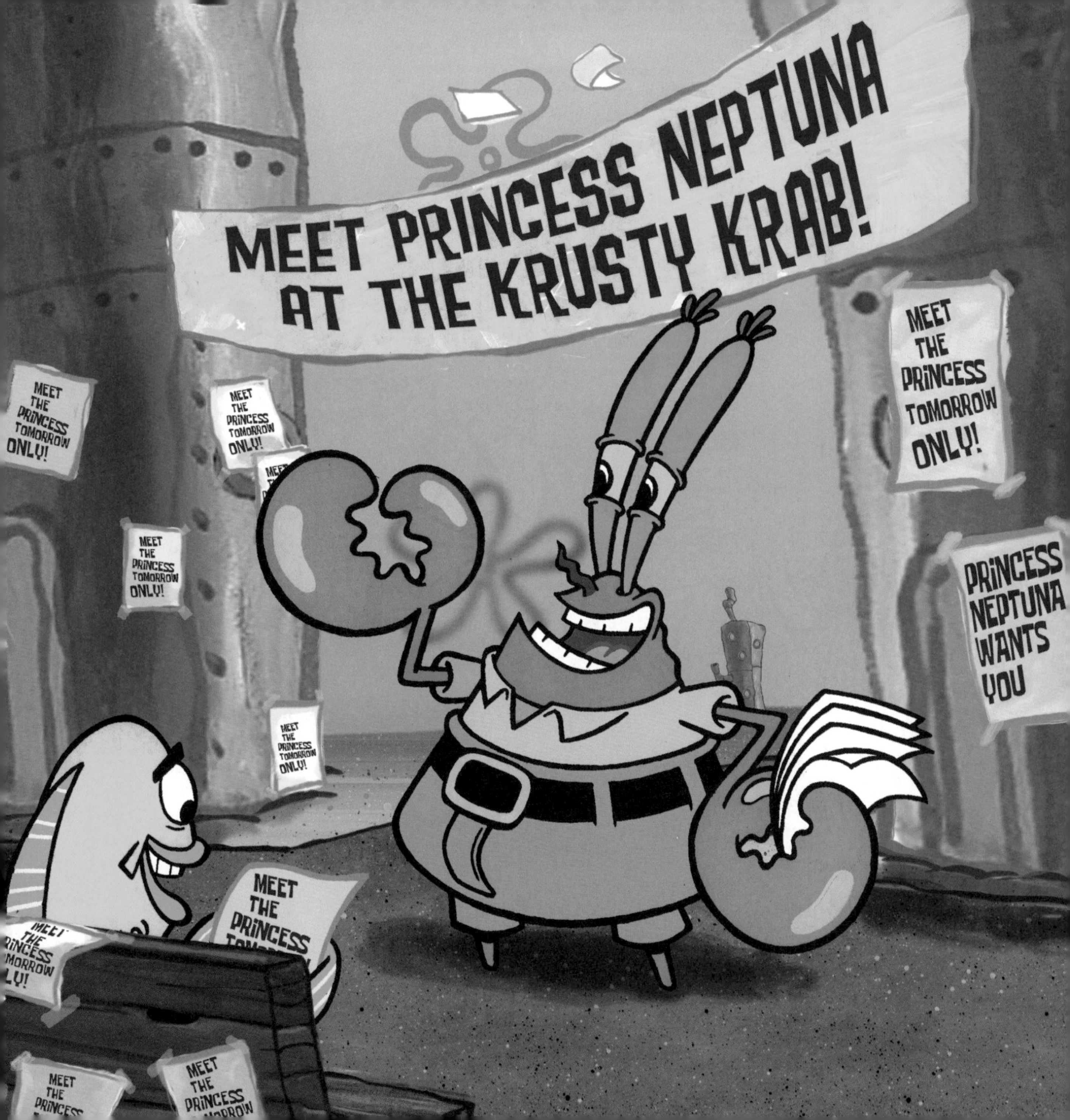
MEET PRINCESS NEPTUNA AT THE KRUSTY KRAB!
MEET THE PRINCESS TOMORROW ONLY!
MEET THE PRINCESS TOMORROW ONLY!
MEET THE PRINCESS TOMORROW ONLY!
MEET THE PRINCESS TOMORROW ONLY!
MEET THE PRINCESS TOMORROW ONLY!
PRINCESS NEPTUNA WANTS YOU

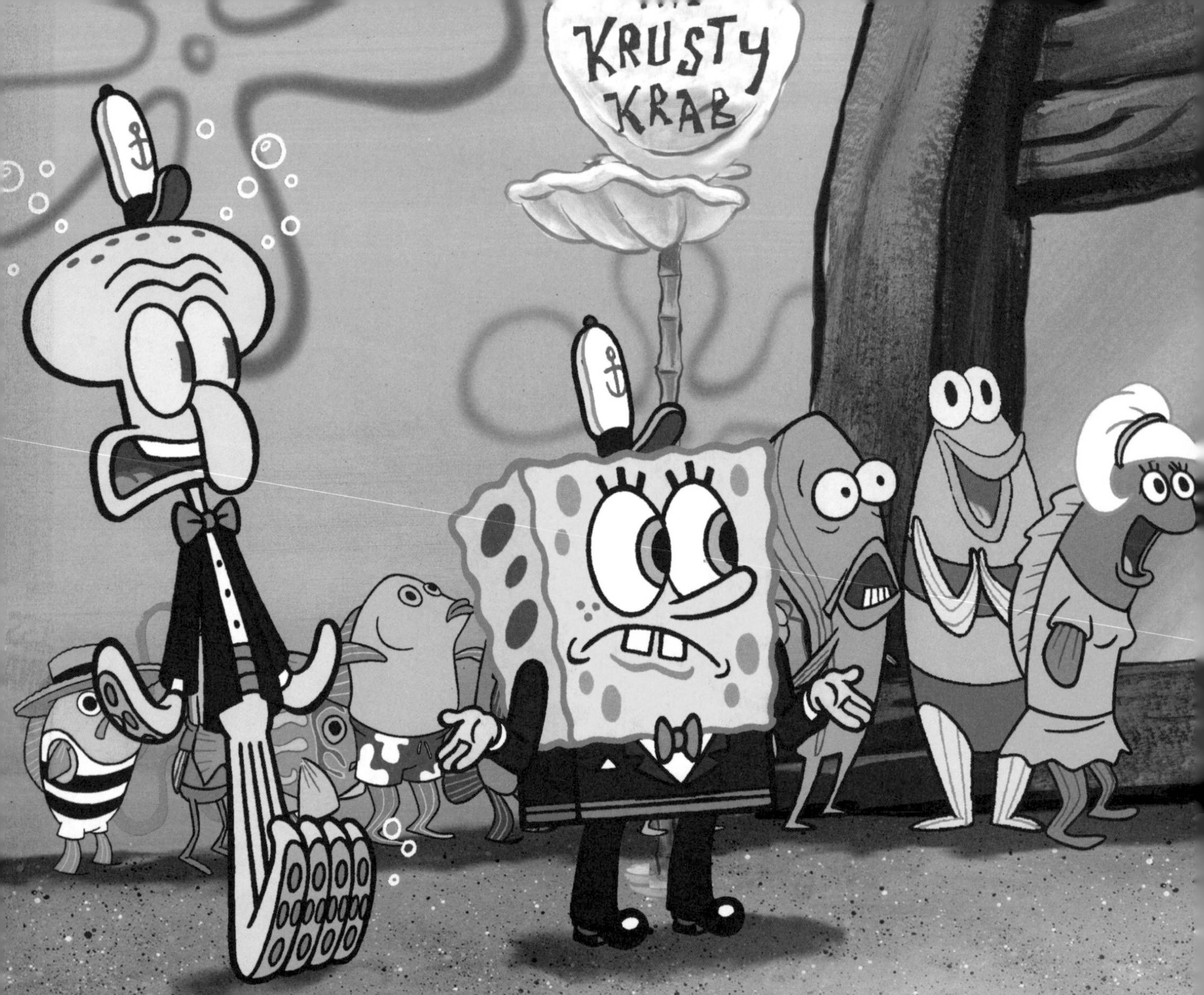
KRUSTY
KRAB

As SpongeBob approached the Krusty Krab the next morning, he saw almost all of Bikini Bottom waiting outside. "Gee," he said, "there sure are a lot of people hungry for delicious Krabby Patties today."

Just then Squidward showed up. "Oh, no!" he cried. "They must all be here to see Princess Neptuna!"

He angrily turned to SpongeBob. "You blabbed to everyone about the princess!"

"No, Squidward," answered SpongeBob. "I was over at your house, remember?"

Squidward scrunched up his face in confusion. "Then how did they all find out?"

"RIGHT THIS WAY!" barked Mr. Krabs. "THIS WAY TO SEE THE PRINCESS! CUSTOMERS WITH MONEY ONLY!"

The truck from the day before pulled up. An eager SpongeBob ran over, "When will the princess be here?" he whispered.

The driver scratched his head and gave SpongeBob a blank look.

"Yesterday you told me to tell Mr. Krabs, 'A princess will be here tomorrow,'" explained SpongeBob.

The driver stared at SpongeBob and then started laughing. "I said, '*The Princess delivery* will be here tomorrow.' Y'know, *Princess Napkins.*"

SpongeBob's mouth dropped open. "You mean Princess Neptuna isn't coming?"

"Nope," the driver replied, unloading several boxes onto the ground. "But here are your napkins. See ya!"

SpongeBob stared at the boxes. "What good are napkins when I promised everyone a princess?" he thought aloud.

SpongeBob spotted Patrick walking by. "Patrick!" he said. "Am I glad to see you! I need you to dress up as the princess again to fool that big crowd of customers!"

Patrick shook his head. "No way, SpongeBob. Last night you said I looked funny."

"Yeah, but . . . but," said SpongeBob, sputtering.

"No buts about it," said Patrick stubbornly. "I'm not going to look ridiculous in front of all those people." And he put on his beanie propeller hat and turned to walk away.

"But, Patrick," SpongeBob begged, "who am I going to get to be the princess?"

"Hello, loyal subjects from Bikini Bottom!" SpongeBob called to the crowd. "I am your princess!"

Everyone turned and stared at SpongeBob. "That's Princess Neptuna?" someone shouted.

"Of course I am!" squeaked SpongeBob. "Well, it's sure been great to see you. And now if you'll excuse me . . ."

"THAT'S NOT PRINCESS NEPTUNA!" said a guy with a very loud voice. "THAT'S JUST SOME GUY DRESSED UP IN A PRINCESS COSTUME!"

The crowd murmured angrily.

"GET HIM!" they yelled. Everyone started to rush toward SpongeBob!

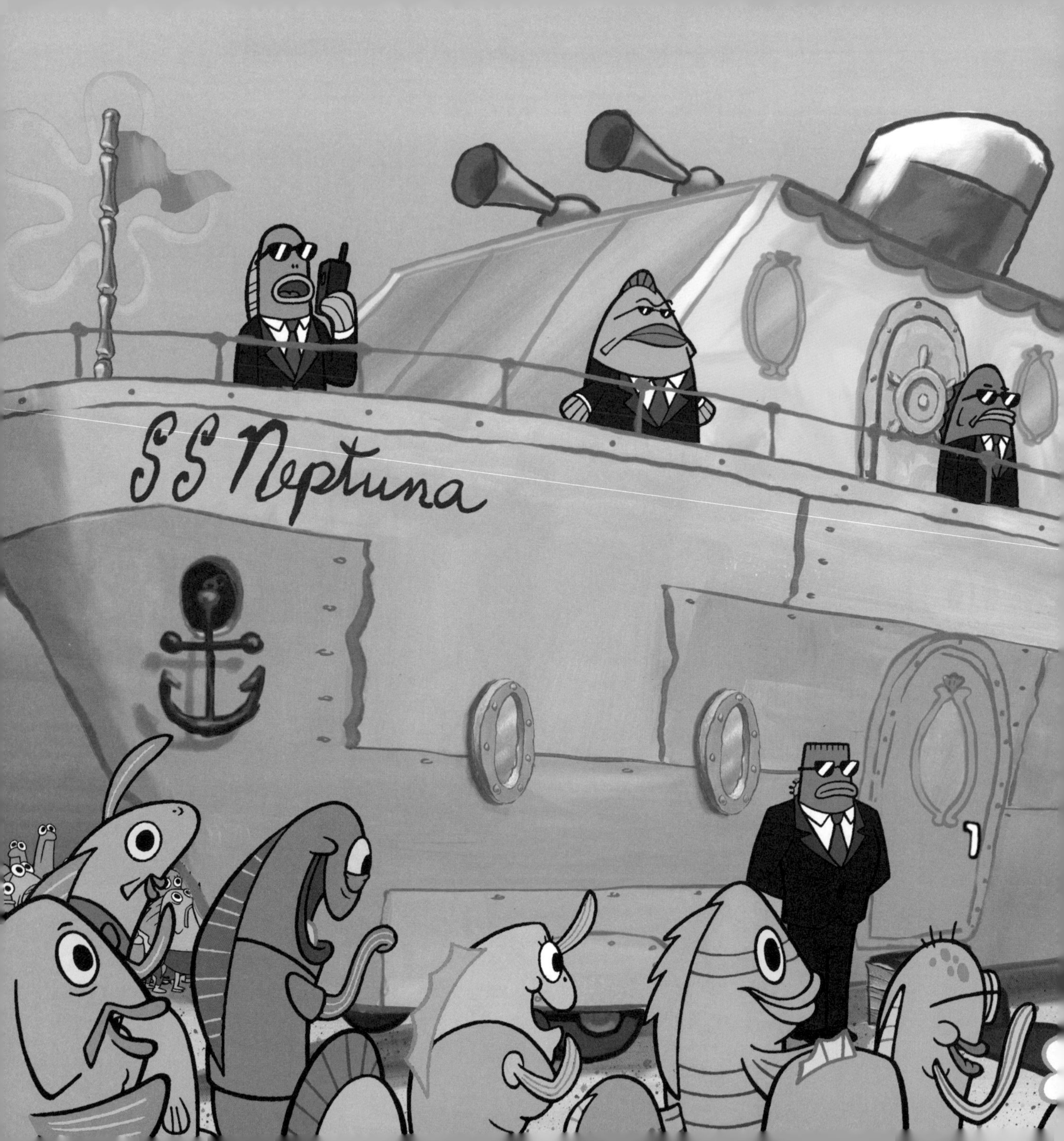
SS Neptuna

Before the crowd reached SpongeBob, a magnificent boat pulled up. The door opened, and a princess climbed out. "Hello, everyone," she said, smiling and waving. "I'm Princess Neptuna."

SpongeBob hoped he could remember the royalty lessons Squidward had given him. He bowed several times and got down on one knee. Taking her hand in his, SpongeBob said, "Hello, Princess Neptuna, what brings you to our humble establishment, the Krusty Krab?"

"Well," she answered, "I saw the crowd, so I stopped to see what was going on. I just *love* crowds!"

Princess Neptuna signed autographs for everyone–including Squidward. She even tried a Krabby Patty. "This Krabby Patty is a delicious morsel, SpongeBob," she said. "But it's a little messy."

SpongeBob brought over a box. "How would you like your very own box of Princess Napkins?" he asked.

The princess smiled. "You sure know how to treat a princess, SpongeBob!"

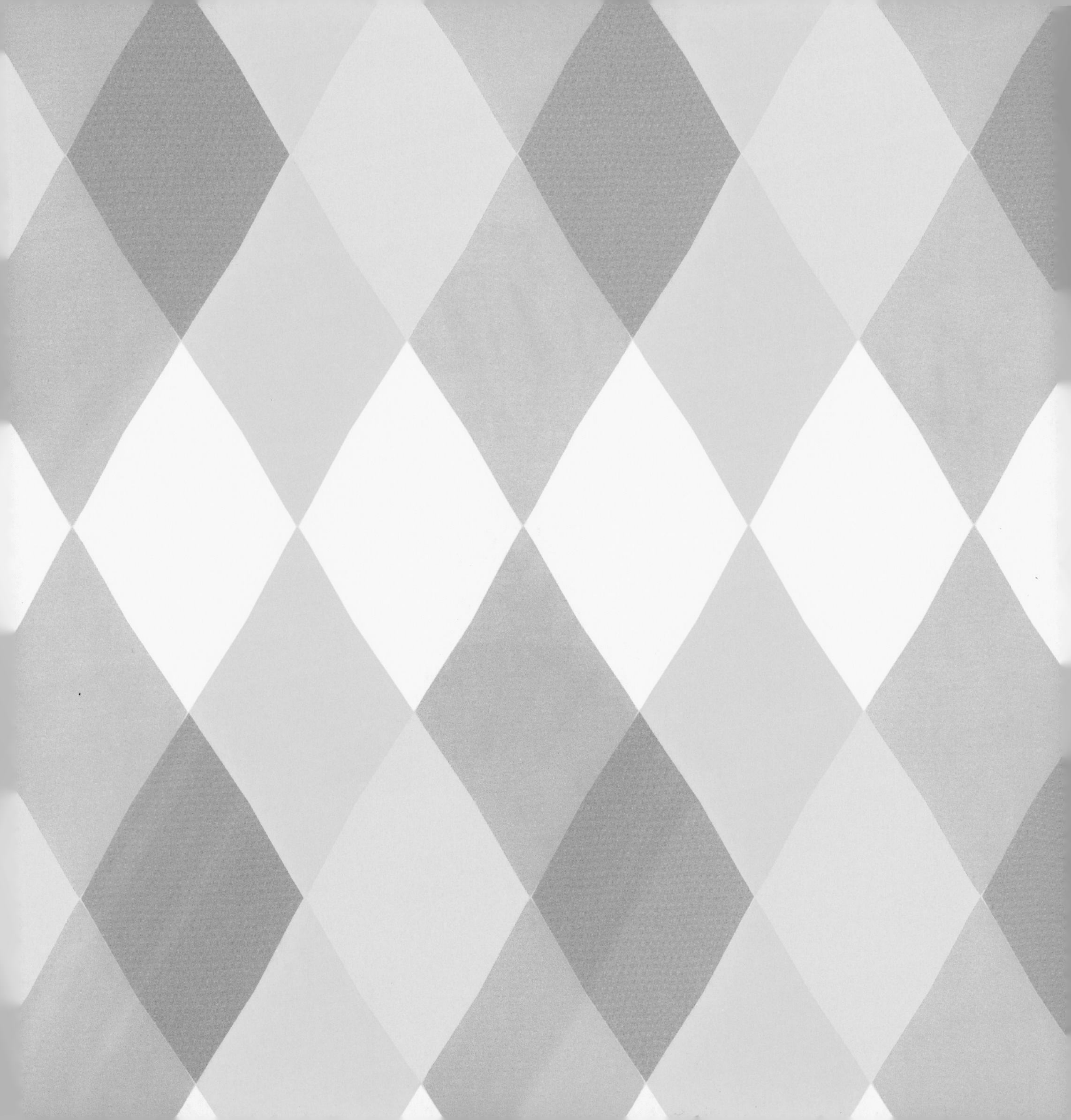

A Medieval Adventure

by Steven Banks

illustrated by The Artifact Group

SpongeBob and Patrick hurried through Bikini Bottom to get to Medieval Moments restaurant.

"C'mon, Patrick, it's almost time for the joust!" said SpongeBob. The two friends stood before the entrance.

A booming voice played over the castle's speakers. "You're just twenty wizard's paces away from swords, sorcery, and bad hygiene!"

The restaurant's stadium was packed with a cheering audience. The medieval king cleared his throat and spoke into a microphone. "By royal decree, I ask that two people come forth for the royal joust!"

SpongeBob and Patrick waved their hands wildly. "Over here! Pick us!" they cried. The king called them into the arena.

"I can't believe we'll be watching the royal joust from so close up!" SpongeBob said.

"You are not watching the joust," an attendant remarked. "You are *in* the joust!"

SpongeBob and Patrick nervously climbed on to their seahorses. "Mr. Seahorse, sir . . . , you're gentle on beginners, aren't you?" SpongeBob whispered. Suddenly, both seahorses bucked up into the air.

"SpongeBob, HELP!" yelled Patrick. The boys flew off the seahorses and crashed through the wall!

PLOP! SpongeBob and Patrick hit the ground.

"Look, Patrick!" said SpongeBob. An army of knights was charging toward them. "Some employees from the restaurant are coming to help us!"

"Arrest them for committing the act of witchcraft by falling from the sky!" ordered one of the knights. "Taketh them to jail!"

"Wow, they really go the extra mile here!" SpongeBob said.

In the royal dungeon, SpongeBob and Patrick heard a familiar sound . . . it was bad clarinet playing!

"Squidward? What are you doing here?" asked SpongeBob.

"My name is Squidly!" said the prisoner. "I was the royal fool until I told a bad joke and the king locked me up!"

"We really *are* in medieval times!" said SpongeBob. "We must have gone back to the past!"

Suddenly, they felt a rumble in the dungeon. "That is the evil wizard's dragon sent to destroy the king's village," explained Squidly.

Then a guard came and took them all to King Krabs.

"Mr. Krabs?" asked SpongeBob.

"I am the feared ruler of this kingdom!" said the king. "I know you have been sent by Planktonamor to destroy me! It is time for your punishment. Off with their heads!"

"Aaah!" cried SpongeBob and Patrick.

"Wait, Father! Spare them!" the king's daughter, Princess Pearl, begged. "Hast thou forgotten the famous prophecy?"

"What prophecy?" asked King Krabs.

Pearl told the story about how two brave knights were supposed to fall from the sky and slay the dragon of Planktonamor, the evil one-eyed wizard!
"Don't you see? These strangers have been sent to rescue us!" Pearl cried.

Suddenly, a huge jellyfish dragon crashed through the castle and grabbed Princess Pearl!

"Help me, Father!" screamed Princess Pearl.

"Let go of her, you overgrown amoeba!" shouted King Krabs.

"The evil Planktonamor's dragon has taken Pearl!" cried King Krabs. "And he won't return her until I give him my kingdom!"

"Bummer," said Patrick.

"You two brave knights have been chosen to rescue Princess Pearl!" ordered King Krabs.

"We're ready, Your Majesty!" said SpongeBob.

"And take my fool, Squidly, with you!" added the king.

Giveth Me Your Kingdom!

The trio first stopped at the local blacksmith to get proper armor for the trip. "We have a long journey ahead of us," said Squidly.

SpongeBob reached inside his pocket and pulled out a brown bag. "I always carry some delicious Krabby Patties with me," said SpongeBob. "After we rescue the princess we'll have a snack."

"Ooooh!" said Patrick.

Soon SpongeBob, Patrick, and Squidly came face to face with the fearsome dark knight who guarded the bridge to Planktonamor's castle.

"None shall pass!" the dark knight boomed.

"But, we have to pass, oh scary knight who looks a lot like my friend Sandy," said SpongeBob. "The king has sent us to rescue the fair Princess Pearl from the evil Planktonamor!"

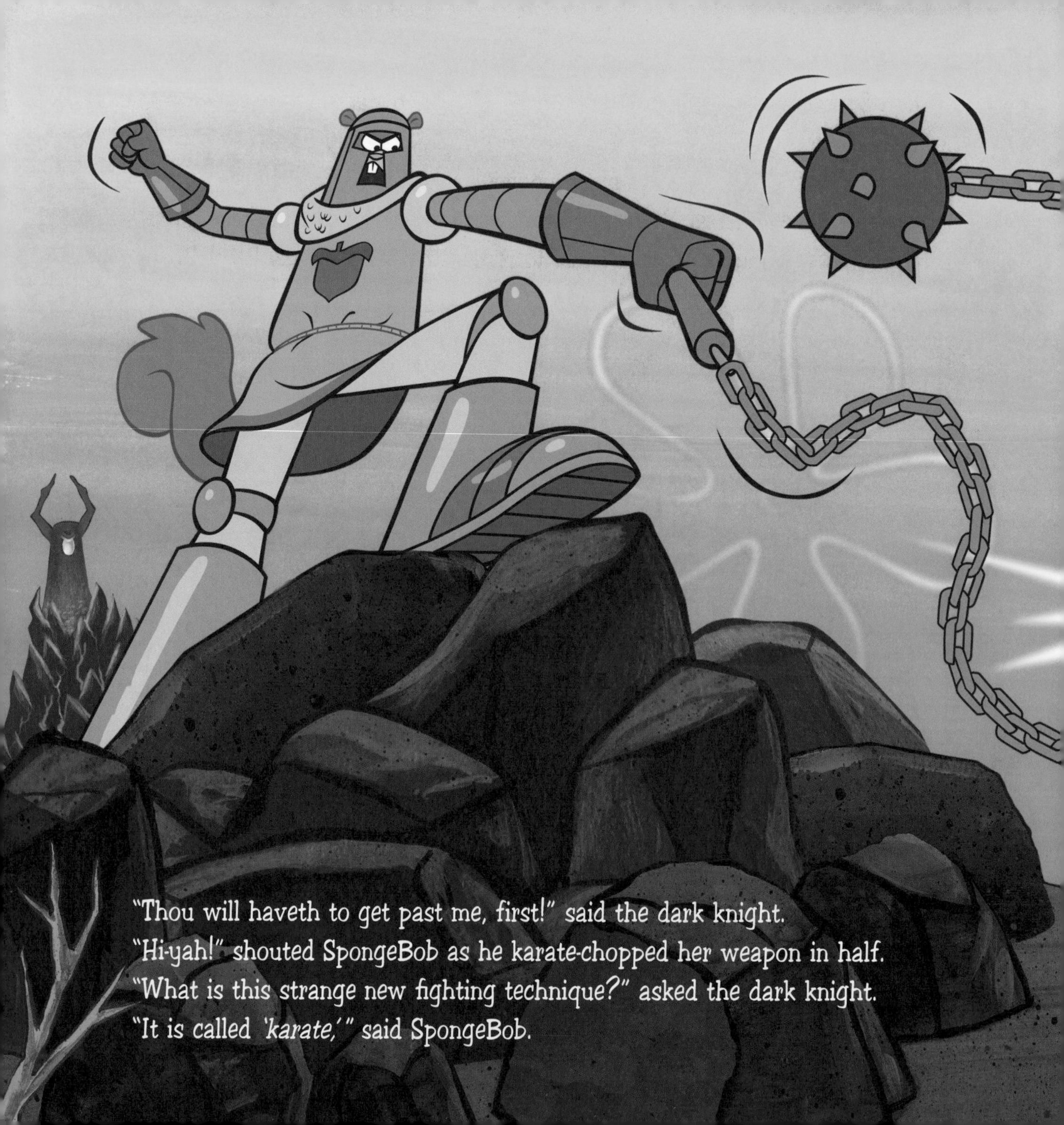

"Thou will haveth to get past me, first!" said the dark knight.
"Hi-yah!" shouted SpongeBob as he karate-chopped her weapon in half.
"What is this strange new fighting technique?" asked the dark knight.
"It is called *'karate,'*" said SpongeBob.

"It pleases me!" said the dark knight. The two fought in a series of karate battles and SpongeBob won.

"Since you have bested me in battle and spared my life, I shall let you all cross, and I shall accompany you on your quest!" said the dark knight.

Meanwhile, in the castle of Planktonamor, the evil wizard was celebrating his upcoming victory. "Ha! Ha! Ha! Soon the king's village will be mine! Mine! Mine!"

"That's what you think!" said Princess Pearl. "The prophecy will come true! My rescuers will save me!"

The dark knight helped SpongeBob, Patrick, and Squidly get past the evil wizard's guards. They climbed up the tower stairs to rescue Princess Pearl.

"Hang on, Princess Pearl! We're coming to help you!" yelled SpongeBob.

"And then we'll eat!" added Patrick.

SpongeBob was determined to stop Planktonamor. "Unhand her, you fiend!" he yelled.

Planktonamor laughed. "Why don't you maketh me?"

"I shalleth!" replied SpongeBob.

"Destroy-eth them, dragon!" ordered Planktonamor.

The giant jellyfish dragon swooped around the castle zapping the intruders.

"I'm afraid this is the end, Patrick!" SpongeBob said, sobbing.

"But I want my Krabby Patty!" cried Patrick.

"Good idea!" said SpongeBob, pulling them out.

Just as Patrick was about to take a bite, the dragon took the food with its tentacle!

"Look! The dragon's eating the Krabby Patty!" exclaimed SpongeBob.

"Hey, dragon!" yelled Planktonamor. "What part of destroyeth dost thou not understand?"

The giant dragon ignored its master and happily kept munching away.

"We defeated the dragon!" shouted SpongeBob.

"Curses!" said Planktonamor. "Foiled by a Krabby Patty!"